New Year's Eve

MARINA ENDICOTT

New Year's Eve

Grass Roots Press

The Good Reads series is funded in part by the Government of Canada's Office of Literacy and Essential Skills.

Grass Roots Press also gratefully acknowledges the financial support for its publishing programs provided by the following agencies: the Government of Canada through the Canada Book Fund and the Government of Alberta through the Alberta Foundation for the Arts.

Alberta
Foundation
for the Arts

Grass Roots Press would also like to thank ABC Life Literacy Canada for their support. Good Reads® is used under licence from ABC Life Literacy Canada.

Library and Archives Canada Cataloguing in Publication

Endicott, Marina, 1958–
    New Year's Eve / Marina Endicott.

(Good reads series)
ISBN 978–1–926583–33–4

    1. Readers for new literates. I. Title. II. Series: Good reads series (Edmonton, Alta.)

PS8559.N475N49 2011   428.6'2   C2011–903262–7

Printed and bound in Canada.

Distributed to libraries and educational and community organizations by
Grass Roots Press
www.grassrootsbooks.net

Distributed to retail outlets by
HarperCollins Canada Ltd.
www.harpercollins.ca

To Peter—
for twenty years, November 4th

Chapter One

The snow started before we left home.

We were supposed to leave at nine that morning, but Grady had worked the night before. And for twelve nights before that. The other guys got time off, but Grady had worked right through Christmas. He was the newest RCMP constable in Drayton Valley, so he got all the rough shifts.

He was supposed to be through at four in the morning, but he didn't make it home till noon. Then he was so tired he had to sleep for a while. The baby was already in her snowsuit. I took her out of it again.

We didn't leave till three. The sun was already fading down the winter sky.

And then when we stopped at Edmonton an hour later for gas, the bank card wouldn't work. I went inside to pay, but it still got declined. I re-counted the days since payday with a shaky feeling in my knees. Then I went back to the car.

"I made a big mistake," I said, when Grady rolled down his window. "I thought today was payday, but it's not till *next* Wednesday."

"Oh, Dixie," he said.

"I'm sorry." I stood there, sick.

"Nothing left in the bank?"

I shook my head. He undid his seat belt. He walked inside, reaching into his wallet for the credit card his dad gave him. "For emergencies," his dad had said. Grady hates using it.

I have to say that Grady did not blame me or say I spent too much money. We just didn't make enough, we both knew that. But I was supposed to keep track.

By the time we left Edmonton, it was getting dark. Five more hours to Saskatoon.

Snow filled the air like feathers from a burst pillow. I never worried while Grady was driving. But with the baby sleeping in the back, the snow scared me.

I looked back to check on her. Sweet flower face in a sea of bright paper. We had packed the Christmas presents for Grady's family around the car seat.

Her lips moved in and out as I watched, as if she was sucking.

"She's hungry even in her sleep," I said.

Grady didn't answer. His eyes were nearly shut against the white glare of snow flying into the windshield.

"We should have left sooner. I'm sorry," I said.

Then I wished I hadn't apologized. We didn't start late because of me.

He shook his head, keeping his eyes on the road. "Not your fault. I couldn't leave the office till I'd finished the paperwork."

That was all we said for a long time.

The sky got darker. The snow fell. The black road ran ahead into the whiteness. At least there was no traffic. Everybody was at a party by this time on New Year's Eve. Only us out on the road, driving and driving.

We were doing okay until the baby started to cry. Sometimes Grady sings to her, but not that night. I turned in my seat to tickle her cheek. I gave her the soother, but she kept spitting it out again.

"Can't you make her shut up?" Grady finally said. He didn't shout, but he was getting tense. The stress of driving in the dark through a cloud of flying white.

"She's hungry," I said. "Sorry." Some days all I ever said was *sorry*. "If I'd fed her just before we left, maybe she would have slept through."

He laughed. "Right. She hasn't slept more than three hours in her whole life."

"Seven, last Sunday!"

He shook his head like he didn't believe me, but he didn't answer.

We were only going 60. At this rate, the trip was going to take forever. I hummed to make the baby stop fussing, giving her my best good-mama smile.

She let the soother fall damply out of her mouth and grinned back at me. Drool ran down her chin. She looked pretty cute, actually. Never thought I'd think that about a drooling baby.

"Daisy, Daisy, give me your answer, do," I sang to her. *"I'm half crazy, all for the love of*

you…" My mom used to sing me that old song all the time.

Daisy's eyes were as dark blue as the night sky out the window. My back hurt, twisting around like that, but she started crying again if I turned away.

Grady pulled off the highway at the next exit and turned the car in at a closed-down gas station. The wheels grated over a pile of hard snow at the edge of the road. Grady likes to be safe. He's seen too many accidents.

"Feed her," he said. Leaving the car running, he made his seat lie back and closed his eyes. "If you weaned her, you know, we could keep going while she had a bottle."

I hate it when he gets impatient like that, when it's about the baby. He's allowed to be crabby with me, but not with her.

I pulled her out of her car seat and lifted my top. She let out little whimpers, as if she was saying, *A breast, thank God, I nearly starved to death.*

I closed my eyes. I couldn't stop nursing yet. It was too soon—she wasn't going to be a year old till June. Then it would be summer, and maybe I would leave Grady and go to Regina with her. I could stay with my dad for a while, till I got a job. So she would still have a father figure. My eyes hurt. I guess I'd been staring into the snow, too. I would not let myself cry.

The baby finished nursing and fell fast asleep. She didn't even stir when I put her back in the car seat.

"Okay," I said to Grady. "She's good. We can go now."

He opened his eyes. He looks so sad when he first wakes up. I think he has bad dreams all the time. After rolling his head right and left, he pulled the seat up straight again, but he didn't start driving.

At the edge of the road, a sign shining in the headlights said: "Two Hills 32 km."

"Two Hills," Grady said. "That's where Ron Cox is now."

Ron and Grady had trained together at Depot Division in Regina. Being in the same training troop is a big deal for Mounties. Six months of getting whipped into shape together makes a bond.

Ron and Grady ended up near each other for their first postings, too, in small towns close to Edmonton. Ron at Westlock and Grady at Drayton Valley. When Ron got married to Sharla, Grady was his best man. Ron had been moved to Two Hills last year.

The storm was worse. We stared out the windshield at the snow. A million sparks of white hid the road.

"I don't think I can drive through this any more," Grady said. "We could make it to Two Hills. It's New Year's Eve, let's go have a party with Ronny."

Cheered up all of a sudden, Grady got out and ran through the snow to phone Ron from the gas station phone booth. That's what men do for each other. Or maybe I mean, that's what friends do for each other. They're good friends. You've got to have friends.

I put on some hand cream. My makeup was in my suitcase, somewhere under the Christmas presents. Sharla takes good care of herself. She's always nicely dressed. I was in sweats, as usual.

Grady came back, nodding. "They're home. Ron says come on over."

"Great," I said, trying to be nice. I reached over to touch his cheek.

He pulled back, screwing up his nose. "What's that stink on your hands?"

He does have a very sensitive nose.

You have to be patient.

But you also have to figure out the difference between being patient and being a doormat. When you have a daughter watching you.

Chapter Two

You could see right away that Sharla was not happy to see us.

Ron cried, "Grady! Grade-*A!* You *bugger!* Come on in!"

Sharla just stood by the kitchen island, waiting.

"Nice place," Grady said, looking around. Smiling now, in the warmth. "You lucked out here!"

The house was big. Open plan, lots of wood cabinets. A long island with a granite top between the kitchen and the living room. Velour recliners with drink holders, giant TV. *Wheel of Fortune* was on.

"Built the house last year—before that we were in the barracks. Or what used to be the barracks, in the old days. It was bad, eh, Sharla?" He laughed, she didn't. "But Sharla's dad is a builder. He came for three months, and we put in some sweat, got 'er up in no time."

Linoleum in the kitchen, beige carpet everywhere else. I would have gone for hardwood if it had been our house. Except of course our house was old and rented, my dad not being a builder. Not one to hand out emergency credit cards, either. But he had stopped drinking. So if I decided to take Daisy to live in Regina, staying with my dad might be okay.

I stood on the mat by the door, holding the baby in her car seat. I hadn't taken off my boots, so I didn't dare move. Sharla is a major bitch, if you ask me. Lucky nobody asked.

"Wow, Dixie!" Ron said, catching sight of the car seat. "Who's this?"

Ron's a nice guy. I pulled back the blanket so he could peek at the baby.

Daisy's hat had come undone. Under it her red hair was damp and curly. Little finger ringlets. My mom would have loved her hair.

"Look at that! Would you look at that—look, Sharla! What a princess!" Ron glanced up quick, to check that it was a girl.

I nodded and grinned at him.

Ron was shorter than Grady. Short for a Mountie, but in good shape, with a thick cap of brown hair and a nice sense of humour. I liked Ron.

At their wedding and every time we'd met since, Sharla had spoken to me exactly zero times.

"What's the baby's name?" Ron asked.

"Daisy," I said. "She's called Daisy."

Sharla laughed.

I could see she thought naming a baby Daisy was stupid.

We had meant to call her Ruth Anne, after Grady's mom and mine. But after she was born, she opened her eyes, dark sky blue, and stared up at me. I knew right away her name was Daisy. Grady had been sitting beside my hospital bed in his uniform. People probably thought I was under arrest. He said, "Are you nuts? *Daisy?*" Then he got called out. So I filled out the forms by myself, and I named her Daisy.

Now Grady sang to her, *"I'm half crazy, all for the love of you..."*

He couldn't be kind to me, but he could be soft to the baby. We did that a lot. Talked to each other through her.

"Wait till she opens her eyes," I told Ron. "You'll see, it suits her."

Ron gave me a quick hug, around the car seat. He was in uniform, and the police radio sat on the counter. That meant he was on duty, even on New Year's Eve.

"Come on, sit, sit," he said. He took the car seat while I got my coat and boots off.

Sharla said, "I need another cooler! You, Grady?"

Grady shrugged. She gave him a vodka cooler, but he didn't open it. Ron was not drinking, so Grady wouldn't, either. He was polite about keeping people company. He didn't even like to eat a sandwich while I sat without one. Eating every time he did was making me fat. Or Daisy was doing it. Something was making me pretty huge.

I said no thanks when Sharla finally shoved a cooler toward me. The doctor said it's okay to have a drink once in a while. Even Grady's mom said a beer at supper would help with nursing. But I didn't like it any more. Couldn't drink coffee, either, since I got pregnant. If someone cooked bacon, I had to leave the house.

Even now, the chicken wing smell from the oven was making me a bit queasy.

"To what do we owe the honour," Sharla said, still leaning her hip against the island. Not asking a question, just making us feel stupid for coming by. She had on a purple velvet dress. Her bare legs were fake tanned, and she had little diamonds pasted on her toenails. Her blonde hair fell in soft curls like she'd had it done at a beauty salon. She must have used a ton of hairspray.

"You've got a party going on here," I said. There were chips and dip, M&M food boxes by the sink, platters all over the island. "We can't crash the party, Grady. We ought to get back on the road pretty quick."

"No, no!" Ron popped open a beer and gave it to Grady. "A couple of people were coming over—but the snow's stopped most of them. And I'm on duty, as you see. Tim Lamont's gone to Vegas," he told Grady.

"Without Jade," Sharla said.

"He's on a golf trip," Ron said, to excuse Tim for going without his wife.

"Yeah," Sharla said. "*Golfing* in Vegas, I bet."

"You have a three-member detachment here?" Grady asked Ron.

"Yeah, we still have three. Tim and me, and Marie Poirier is the other member. She's out with a broken leg till February."

"Are you still trying to get a transfer?"

"Not now we've built the house," Sharla said. "Anyway, Ron lies down and lets Staffing walk all over him." Her voice had a curling tail in it, a little sting on the end all the time.

Ron laughed again. He laughed the way I said *sorry,* too often and in the wrong places.

But no, that wasn't fair. Grady didn't act anything like Sharla.

"Come see my new truck," Ron said, still laughing. The men disappeared through a door into the heated garage. We could still hear their voices, but not what they said.

"My dad carpeted the garage, around the edges," Sharla said, staring after them. "Pits for three cars. You can change your own oil. It's quite the showplace."

"Wow," I said. "You're lucky."

She looked back at me.

"Want a drink?"

"I can't—I'm nursing," I said. That word *nursing* sounds weird.

"How old is the baby?"

"Um, almost six months."

Sharla leaned over the island, as if she might lean far enough forward to see the baby.

But then she straightened up again.

"Well, *I* can have a drink," she said. "How about a pop?"

Being with her was hard. She was all jagged edges. Maybe she just didn't like me for some reason. Maybe I reminded her of some girl in grade nine who stole her boyfriend.

"I'm going to—" She stopped talking because Ron's police radio began to squawk.

"Ron!" she shouted, and he poked his head back into the kitchen in time to hear it.

"Alpha 22, Alpha 22," the radio voice said. "10-71… I have a caller reporting loose animals.

Horses on the road north of town, before the gravel pit turnoff. Copy?"

Ron hit the button and talked to the Control person. He said he'd head out and check. We knew a guy in Drayton Valley who had been killed when he hit a horse on the road. Moose are even worse. Their legs are so long that their bodies smash over the hood of the car, right through the windshield.

As Ron was talking, Grady came in from the garage. He set his still-full beer in the sink and picked up his coat. "I'll go, too," he told Ron. "If there's a few horses loose, you could use a hand."

Ron said sure, and they got their boots on.

I was giving Grady the bug-eyed beg: *Please please don't leave me alone with Sharla!* But he avoided my eyes. Laughing to himself, he bent over to do up his boots. I was mad at him, but it *was* kind of funny.

They left.

Cold air ran into the room, and a flurry of snow.

"Jeez! Shut that door!" Sharla was used to telling people what to do, boy.

I went to shut it.

"Fuck, it's cold," she said.

Around our house we had stopped swearing. You can't tell what words the baby will pick up.

"You need a shawl or something," I told her. That sounded kind of rude. I added, "Nice dress, though, Sharla."

"Yeah," she said. She laughed. Ron not being there to laugh for her. "My Christmas present to myself."

"Wow. Nice, a nice colour on you."

No blonde should ever wear purple, in my opinion

I looked at the TV instead. The *Wheel of Fortune* boxes read:

__v__r s t a y y__u r w __ l c __m__

"I'd like to buy an O!" shouted a giggly woman on the show.

Vanna touched the first box, and two more. Now the letters spelled:

o v __ r s t a y y o u r w __ l c o m __

The woman cried, "Is there a K?"

She'd kick herself for that later.

Chapter Three

"Maybe you should get the baby off the tit," Sharla said. People without kids are always giving you advice, I notice.

She had six shot glasses lined up on the counter, filled with bright stuff.

"Jell-O shooters," she said. "Don't you have some of that formula stuff to give her just this once? You'd be more fun at a party if you were drinking, too."

I put my coat over a chair. I couldn't escape now that Grady had gone off with Ron. "How about a beer? I could finish Grady's beer."

Sharla clapped her hands and cheered.

She handed me a fresh beer from the fridge and knocked back a green Jell-O shot to celebrate. Then she had a red shot and shook her head fast, so her cheeks jiggled. It was funny.

"Plus, what you were you thinking?" she asked me. "Daisy and Dixie? Ha!"

"Well, she's not going to call me Dixie, she'll call me Mom or something."

"Did you get called Dixie Cup at school?"

I couldn't help laughing. "Yes! And D Cup. That wasn't as bad as them singing *I wish I was in Dixie...*"

"Isn't there a Daisy song, too?"

"Yeah," I said. "I checked it, though, I don't think there's anything bad in it."

"You'd be surprised," Sharla said. "A girl in my class, Theresa Doherty, her parents wouldn't have thought there was anything wrong with that. But she got called Turdo all through school."

Sharla was making me laugh on purpose. Weird. I wondered what she wanted. Maybe just company.

"And her poor brother Dilbert..."

She must be drunk already, I thought. At her wedding she was Ice Princess Barbie, frozen in a full ball dress. She hadn't cracked a joke or a smile all that night. Living out in the wilderness must be good for her.

The radio crackled. We could hear the guys out there somewhere.

"Control?" Ron was laughing into the radio. "This is Alpha 22. It's not horses on the road, it's *buffalo*. They're just north of town. Three of them."

Control's answer was lost in static.

"Yeah," Ron said. "The rancher is on scene. The buffalo are moving south toward town. Could I get you to contact Fish and Wildlife Services, see who they've got around? We could use some extra hands."

"10-4, Alpha 22," Control came through.

In the background you could hear Grady shouting, "Watch out! Watch that one go!"

Great. They'd be out all night, I thought. Dancing with buffalo.

The radio crackled off. Sharla picked up four more shooters, two in each hand. "They'll be farting around out there for hours, waiting for the fish cops to show," she said. "I'm going in the hot tub. Come on. Bring your beer."

I picked up Daisy's car seat and followed.

The hot tub had steamed up the closed-in sunroom at the back of the house. All I could see outside the sliding glass doors was more snow. The water smelled clean. Ron was a neat freak. If Grady and me had a hot tub, it would stink. Both of us waiting for the other one to clean it.

I set the car seat close to the tub and turned down Daisy's blanket. Under her tight-closed eyes, her round cheeks were as smooth as pudding.

"Cute," Sharla said. "Where'd she get the red hair from?"

"That happens," I said. "When one parent is blonde and the other has darker hair."

Sharla laughed. "Okay, okay! I'm not saying you cheated on Grady! You'd be a fool to do that."

I stood by the edge of the tub. The bright blue water was still, but clouds of steam swirled on the surface. There were lights under the water. No way I was getting in there.

Sharla flicked switches to turn up the heat in the room. "We should eat the caramel apple pie. It won't keep. Nobody else is coming to the party, looks like."

"I guess I am a little hungry," I said. Now that she'd mentioned pie, I was starving.

As if I hadn't answered, she started stripping her purple dress off. She dropped it on the cedar floor, then her sparkly necklace. I was glad to see that she had a black spandex thing on, like a bathing suit.

There was a big TV in there, too, mounted high up on the wall. *Biggest Loser* was on. The contestants were talking about their love lives. "I was so shy, my wife had to propose," said a huge guy, his limp hair parted in the middle. "Or I'd still be single."

"Single. Lucky him," Sharla said, and hit the clicker to turn the TV off. She made a moaning noise as she slipped into the hot water.

The beer was good. Cool, in this steaming hot room. I sat on the edge of the hot tub.

"For Pete's sake, get in," Sharla said. She knocked back another shooter. "Aren't you cold out there?"

"I don't have a bathing suit."

Sharla shrugged, her shoulders lifting out of the water to make ripples. "Take off your socks and sit on the edge, it'll warm you up."

I was still cold from the drive. I pulled off my socks and rolled up my sweat pants.

The edge was sharp. It dug into my butt no matter how I sat. But the water was hot, hot, hot. I bent to let my hands dangle in the heat. It felt good.

"Oh, come on, take your sweat pants off at least. The water's so good…"

I couldn't.

"Too chicken?"

"Too fat to get in a hot tub," I said. "Still haven't lost the baby weight."

"You look okay. You're not that much bigger than you were at my wedding."

I must have looked mad, or sad, or something. There was a pause. I thought she was going to apologize. But no.

"Are you and Ron going to have kids?" I asked.

She drank another vodka shot, her last one. Four empty glasses in a row on the edge of the tub.

"I've had three miscarriages so far," Sharla said.

I didn't dare look at her.

"They just keep dying on me," she said.

I had no idea what to say.

After a minute I stood up and pulled off my sweat pants. I got down into the water with her.

"Sorry," I finally said. "I'm really sorry."

"Yeah. The first was the day before my wedding. That was fun. Another last summer. Lost the third one just before Christmas."

She leaned over the edge and stared at Daisy's upturned sleeping face.

"She is pretty cute," Sharla said.

Then she jumped out of the tub, grabbed a towel, and ran across the tiles, leaving damp footprints. "Shit! I forgot the wings!"

Chapter Four

The chicken wings were good. Not too burnt. Sharla brought them on a tray and we ate them while we sat in the water.

After that, the hot tub was too hot. Even the room was too hot.

"Let's go over to the town hall," Sharla said. "It's just across the road."

I had leaned out of the tub to check on Daisy. Still sleeping. Sometimes I want to wake her up and play with her. But that is never a good idea.

"What's over there?"

"Community dance," Sharla said. "Ron doesn't go to dances. If you party with people, it's harder to arrest them when they're driving home drunk. But we could go, by ourselves."

"I can't go in sweats. I'd have to get my suitcase from the car," I said.

Sharla said she had stuff that might fit me.

The master bedroom had a huge bathroom off it, with twin sinks and a Jacuzzi tub. Sharla and Ron must spend a lot of time in water, I thought. A lot of mirrors, too. Sharla didn't have to avoid them, and Ron didn't seem like the vain type. He was okay-looking. But you noticed how nice he was before anything else. Like a big nose or a mole, his kindness stuck out.

Sharla pulled rodeo-style shirts and jeans out of the closet, checking which looked best in the mirror. She shoved a pair of jeans at me, new, with the tags still on.

"Got these at Winners in Edmonton last fall, they're *way* too big for me. Before they changed their take-back rules."

"I'll pay you," I said. Then I remembered that I had no money.

"Don't bother," she said. "They were, like, ten bucks. Good if somebody can use them."

I was very relieved. And the jeans even fit. The zipper did up without too much straining.

The shirt had pearl buttons that were actually snaps. As soon as I did them up, they snapped open again.

"I'll wear the shirt open," I said, giving up. I pulled my spare t-shirt out of Daisy's diaper bag.

Sharla was busy putting on mascara. Her mouth pulled down to stretch her eyes open. She said *mm-hmm,* and did the other eye. A big makeup case sat on the bathroom counter. Eighteen eye shadow colours, about forty lipsticks and blushes.

She made me sit on a stool while she made up my face.

"You're good at this." I tried to speak without blinking.

"I thought about being a makeup artist," she said. "Like for the movies? But my dad wanted me to be a dental hygienist."

She did have really white teeth.

"Are you working now?"

"Part time, two days a week. I don't like the dentist, though."

This was pretty weird, to be having an ordinary conversation with Sharla.

She turned me so I could see myself in the mirror. She'd done a good job.

Then she brushed my hair out and pinned up a couple of twists, so most of it was piled on my head. With the curling iron, she caught some smaller strands. In no time, I had little ringlets falling on each side.

It was the best I'd looked in years. All sparkling. And I liked those jeans, they made me feel trim.

"Good," she said, turning me from side to side. She sprayed my hair like crazy.

Then she turned aside and went to the bedroom, stripping off her towel and bodysuit on the way. She picked a new bra and socks from a drawer. I felt pretty awkward being there while she wandered around naked. She paid no attention to me at all. I couldn't help seeing that the rug did not match the curtains, if you know what I mean. So the blonde hair was a dye job. But she had smooth, unstretched skin and nice little unsaggy breasts.

I turned to the baby so I didn't have to watch Sharla.

Daisy was awake, beginning to move her head from side to side. She reminded me of her dad, waking up.

I undid the straps and took Daisy out of the car seat, holding her tight. We walked in front of the long mirror.

I'd been in maternity jeans for more than a year. The ones I had on now were my first pair without a wide band of elastic across the belly. Zipped up snug over my pale leftover baby flab, the jeans looked good.

"Okay!" Sharla said, pulling a rodeo belt tight around her tiny waist. The shiny buckle was bull-rider size, as big as a pie plate. "Let's get over there, get this party started!"

I changed Daisy's diaper and put her in a clean sleeper and back into her snowsuit. She didn't like that too much. She waved her arms around and said *Nahh!* in little explosions. One of her kicks got me straight in the jaw. But I was the boss of her, and we were going to the dance.

Sharla found a blanket to fold around Daisy. We wrapped scarves up to our eyes, but it was still cold. Ice under the snow made me slide a couple of times, but we got there.

Trucks filled the parking lot by the hall, and more were parked along the road. A yellow light bulb lit up the front door, where people were going in and out.

Inside, the hall was hot, with more of those yellow lights glowing. People stood in bunches around the bar and the food table. Fewer out on the dance floor, but enough. It was noisy.

"Hey, there's Jade," Sharla said. "Jade!" she called "Jade!"

A woman waved and came toward us. A fringed jacket hung easy over her wide shoulders. As she walked the fringes swayed a little.

Sharla spoke in my ear. "Jade—she's Tim Lamont's wife. He's the Mountie in charge here. The one who went to Vegas without her."

Jade was taller than me, with long dark hair. She was really good looking. She looked like the woman jeans were invented for. I felt young and shy and stupid.

But she smiled at me with an open face when Sharla said who I was. About the snowstorm and why we were there. Jade gave me a hug, for nothing.

Then I forgot how beautiful she was and just liked her.

Good thing I did. Because Sharla, again, was not too friendly.

"Why don't you like her?" I asked Sharla when Jade went back to her table to get her drink.

Sharla shrugged. "I never said I didn't. She's bossy, I guess."

Sometimes people see their own faults in other people.

I set Daisy's car seat on the table so she could see the dancers. I rocked the seat gently to the music.

An older guy stopped beside Sharla. He bent his head to speak, and she went off with him. They joined the two-stepping couples on the dance floor. I could never get the hang of the two-step. I always turned it into a waltz by mistake.

Up on a small platform behind the dancers, the little band was not bad. Five or six old guys. They played country tunes, some newer. But not very new. "Achy Breaky Heart," for instance, which was old when I was a kid.

Jade came back and sat on the edge of the table by Daisy, putting her fringed jacket on the chair. At the neck of her soft denim shirt, her collarbone showed like a smooth stick.

"What a cute baby," she said. "How old?"

We talked about Daisy and how great she was. Jade showed me her two boys, fifteen and seventeen. They were standing with their friends by the far wall.

She didn't look old enough to have a seventeen-year-old kid. Or even a seven-year-old.

Jade said the best part of kids growing up was not needing sitters any more. We talked about that for a while. How hard it was to find someone you could leave your kids with and not be nervous. She was easy to talk to.

Tim, her husband, was having a good time in Vegas, she said. "He's been having a hard year. Needed to get away from all this. Be by himself."

Talking about her sons, her face had lit up. When she talked about her husband, the light went out. She looked sad.

I wondered what was going on with Grady and Ron and the buffalo.

Then I realized why I was thinking about them. Because of the lights. Through the window, I could see the rolling red and blue lights of the police cruiser.

I leaned to peer out. They had stopped a truck on the road close to the hall. Ron was standing by the truck window, listening to the driver.

I could see Grady inside the cruiser. Talking into the radio, his face thoughtful in the dashboard light. Seeing him at work always made me like him again. That he would want to do this stupid job.

Chapter Five

Jade asked if she could hold the baby. She lifted Daisy out of the car seat with strong, thin arms. When Daisy stretched out her legs, Jade let her stand up.

I loved to watch Daisy being held by someone else. It was like I could see her better as herself. And she could see me, and that made her happy. She jumped and bent on Jade's knee, dancing to the music. I kind of wanted to dance, too, to try out my new jeans.

A couple of guys asked Jade to dance, but she smiled and said she was taking a break. Everybody gave me a nod of the head or shook my hand. Most people said how cute Daisy was. They were a lot like Drayton Valley people.

"I could use a drink," Jade said.

She got up and handed Daisy over. I was glad to have her in my arms again.

"You?" Jade asked me. "Or are you still nursing?"

I said I was.

"How about soda water with a little cranberry juice in the bottom?" she suggested. "I used to like that."

Jade started for the bar.

Out on the dance floor, someone began shouting. The music broke off, then someone crashed into the band platform. The old guys shrank back to the wall with their instruments.

A couple of kids were yelling at each other. The dancers stood still, watching. Everybody in the hall was watching.

One young guy shouted, "You don't even know who she's—"

The other one swung a punch and connected with a sound like fudge boiling, a wet plop. The first guy went down, out cold.

At that, three or four other kids rushed onto the dance floor and started hitting wildly. The dancers got out of the way, Sharla among them.

The fight looked nothing like a movie. These guys weren't good at fighting, but they really wanted to hurt each other. They grabbed each other, clung together, then swung. They hit too slow or bashed heads. Pretty soon, most of them were bleeding and some of them were crying.

A woman at the table beside us stood up on the bench to take pictures. Tears were running down her face. She kept yelling, "Stop, you boys! Stop them!" Then she'd snap another picture. I think she was the mother of one of the boys.

Sharla worked her way back through the crowd.

I was strapping Daisy back into her seat, figuring that was the safest place. I wanted out of there. Those country fights can get bad fast, because everyone's related.

Somebody smart must have stuck a head out the door and yelled for the cops.

Ron and Grady walked into the back of the hall. They looked really big coming in. Ron still had his long flashlight in one hand.

Grady's navy parka looked like an RCMP coat. But Grady always looks like a policeman. The one you would want to see coming up to the car window after an accident. I think that's why he joined the Mounties.

Ron and Grady made their way up to the dance floor. The crowd parted so they could get through.

Sharla gave me my coat and whispered, "Time to go." Jade tucked the blanket tight around Daisy in the car seat.

Nobody wants the RCMP wives around when people are getting arrested.

The boys had pretty well knocked themselves out already in their fury. One smaller guy still had some fight in him, but Grady held his upper arms in a tight hug. The kid gave up.

We were in the porch of the hall by the time the fighters all came out. I didn't know if Grady saw us as they went by. He was pretty busy.

Somehow he and Ron got all the fighters out to the police cruiser. They fit four of them in the back seat. The father of one of the boys said he'd drive the last two over to the police station. Ron patted his shoulder and said, "See you there."

I hoped this was not going to mean a lot of paperwork.

But of course it would.

Ron and Grady drove away, with the father's truck following.

Chapter Six

Inside the community hall, the music hadn't started up again yet. Outside, the night was quiet and cold. At least the snow had stopped.

This was the wilderness. Fighting and freezing, like in the olden days. The real country started just past Ron and Sharla's place. The lines of parked cars were only temporary. Most days this would be an empty piece of road, going into nowhere.

Jade had gone back into the hall to check on her sons. They came to the door with her. Jade walked over to say goodbye to me and Sharla, the fringes on her jacket swaying.

Softly, so the boys wouldn't hear, Jade said, "They're pretty shocked, but that's good. All those kids will be careful tonight. They say they're going back to Donna's place to have a party with her parents." She turned to me. "Donna's dad is the mayor. They'll be safe."

Sharla's voice sounded loud in the cold, clear air. "Come on with us, Jade. We've got the hot tub going. And there's lots to eat."

For a moment Jade looked at her. "Okay," she said, finally. "Twist my arm."

She waved back to her boys, and we started across the road.

The clouds had parted, and stars were shaken like salt over the black sky. Jade stopped while Sharla lit a cigarette.

I went ahead of them. I was almost across the road.

There was no warning, only a shift in the air. A wind. And the ground shaking.

I thought a truck was coming, but no headlights cut through the night. Was it horses? Suddenly, huge shapes appeared, rushing down the road at me out of the darkness.

A buffalo ran right by me.

Another—oh God, another humped black shape pounding by, too close.

Another one coming—this one was going to run me down. My feet wouldn't move, but I swung the car seat out of its way as far as my arm would reach.

The buffalo changed its path and raced past me. Giant shoulders, narrow pointed feet. A huge bulk, much bigger than I'd ever imagined. The warm depth of brown fur, and the horns. One bright eye, small in the huge head, stared at me. I could see it very clearly in that long half-second.

Daisy swung gently at the end of my left arm. The buffalo ran on, and the wind went with it

Chapter Seven

Jade took the car seat, and Sharla grabbed me before I fell down. The buffalo could have— Daisy could have been killed.

"Fucking shit," Sharla said.

My legs were shaking. I could still feel the pounding in the road.

"I guess the guys didn't get them penned after all," Sharla said. She told Jade about Ron and Grady going out to help the buffalo rancher.

"The fence could have been down somewhere else," Jade said. "Buffalo are smart."

"I wouldn't raise those things for anything." Sharla was right, they ought to be left wild. They always were wild—even behind a fence.

Even when I was so scared, the buffalo had been amazing. To see one so close. I was shivering, but I was not cold.

Jade said, "Everything's okay, Dixie. The baby's okay, you did good. They're gone."

"Yeah. Now all you have to do is walk to the house," Sharla said. "Look, it's, like, twenty more steps."

I thought they might have to carry me. But they wouldn't be able to. I patted at Daisy's blanket and pulled it down to see her face. She opened her eyes and laughed.

"Do it again!" Jade said. "She'd like another ride."

Okay. Okay. We made it up the driveway.

"The thing is," I said, "Grady would kill me if anything happened to Daisy. I mean, I'd kill myself. But he'd come along and dig me up and kill me again."

"She's fine, she's fine," Sharla said. "I'm fucking freezing, though, if you want to know. Come on, come inside."

I stumbled up the steps between the other two and got inside. Now I really wanted a drink.

The house was hot. All the lights blazing. Sharla put the oven on and shoved in a couple more trays of M&M snacks.

Jade and I got our coats off slowly. Daisy sat and bubbled at me. She reached out her arms for me, wanting to nurse. I could feel the milk flooding down into my breasts because of being scared.

I picked Daisy up and went to the velour couch. I sat still, nursing her, stroking her silky hair. The buffalo's thick, curling fur had looked so soft.

Jade said to Sharla, "Looks like you had a party on tonight."

"Not really," Sharla said. "We thought maybe the guys from Smoky Lake detachment would come down. But the snow…"

Sharla seemed a little embarrassed. Like she should have invited Jade, but she hadn't.

They both came and sat on the long couch.

"Over at the dance—what was that fight about?" I asked.

"Who's sleeping with who, of course," Sharla said.

"They were really mad," I said. I felt stupid for saying that. Of course they were mad.

"My kids said it's the new teacher at the high school," Jade said. "She wasn't there, but they say she's having some kind of thing with a student. One of the boys wanted to report her, get her fired. They got worked up. Donna was part of it all, too. She's got a talent for setting people against each other. But she doesn't mean any real harm."

"That girl is a raging bitch," Sharla said.

"Her dad is smart. He's got Donna taking the rest of the kids over to their place. He'll keep them occupied. No more fighting tonight. Just lots of talk."

Sharla got up to make drinks. White Russians this time. Brown Kahlua in the bottom, cold milk on top. Lots of ice. They looked so sweet. My mother didn't nurse me at all, and look, I'm alive. But the books all say you should breastfeed for a solid year. And nursing is easier than washing bottles.

"I do have some powdered baby formula in the diaper bag," I said. "The nurse gave me some free samples and a plastic bottle. I carry the stuff around, just in case, but I've never tried it before."

I looked at Jade. She would know, having two boys.

Jade nodded. "Finish nursing her now, then have a couple of drinks with us. We'll make Daisy a bottle for the morning. You don't have to stop nursing yet, just get her to take a bottle instead sometimes. So you've got the option."

Sharla pulled another glass from the cupboard and shot ice into it from the fridge door. I'll never be rich enough to have a fridge with ice in the door. She poured another drink and put them all on a tray with chips and dip.

"There!" Sharla said. Finally happy, now that I would have a drink. "It'll be waiting for you."

Daisy finished nursing. I changed her diaper and put her in a fresh undershirt. She was happy, too. Fresh and clean and full of milk, she wanted to get down onto the carpet. Jade took her hands and let her stand up and stagger around for a while.

"Okay, ladies," Sharla said. "That hot tub is not going to soak itself."

I took the car seat and Jade brought Daisy. We all went back into the misty sunroom. Sharla put on music and made the jets in the tub whirl the water into froth.

This time I didn't think about it. I stripped off Sharla's shirt and the jeans she'd given me and got into the tub in my underpants and t-shirt.

I took Daisy back from Jade and slid her diaper off. The water was a bit too hot for her, but she could sit on the island of my knee. She loved it.

The other two women stripped down, too. Sharla had no bodysuit this time, and neither did Jade. They just got out of their clothes without thinking about it. Like women in the gym sauna, easy about being naked. I wished I could do that.

They were both pretty in their skin. Sharla pink and gold, thin but soft. She was right to make herself a blonde. It suited her. Jade's dark hair fell over her shoulders and back. She looked like a police woman, like a runner. Strong and lean.

RCMP women, wives and female members, seem to come in two kinds. Thin, strong-willed, and pretty, like these two. Or kind and dumpy, like me.

But Jade was kind, too.

And maybe it's just that all women come in those two types. Hot tub and non–hot tub.

Drinking the White Russian while sitting in the hot water made the treat even colder and sweeter. I stretched it out for as long as I could.

Chapter Eight

It was New Year's Eve, after all. Sharla and Jade talked through what had happened over the last year. I talked a little, too. Where we'd been (me nowhere; both of the others to Vegas). Who had died or got married. The bad and good things.

With a sudden shout, Sharla jumped out of the tub. "Shit, I did it again!"

She grabbed a short terry robe and ran to the kitchen. Whatever she had in the oven smelled good.

"Don't talk about anything interesting while I'm gone!" she yelled back.

That left us with nothing to talk about.

After a minute I said, "Ron told us your husband went to Vegas for some golf."

Jade laughed. "We won a trip in the hospital lottery."

"That was lucky," I said.

She said, "Nah. Who wants heat and sun anyway, when you can have weather like this?"

I shuddered.

"I'm from up north," Jade said. "I don't mind the cold. I'd like to go home to Yellowknife. But it costs too much."

"Do you golf, too?" I asked her.

She laughed again. "No! Tim doesn't either. Golf is just an excuse."

"What's he gone for, then?"

"He's leaving me."

Jade moved in the water. She swept her hair back and leaned her head on one hand. Water dripped from her hand and face.

She corrected herself. "He's thinking about it, about leaving."

I thought she might be crying, but her voice was calm.

I said I was sorry. Looking at her, I couldn't imagine her being left. She was so beautiful. How could he find somebody nicer?

"The boys are old enough now. They'd be okay. It's not like we haven't thought about this before. I used to think about it all the time, when the kids were little. About how I'd leave him. What I'd do. I was going to get a bachelor apartment in Edmonton. I used to look at the apartments for rent section in the newspaper."

I wanted to tell her I did that, too. But it seemed disloyal to Grady, to tell someone that I thought about leaving him. Thought about it pretty much every day.

"What—" I broke off. None of my business.

"What what?" Jade flicked water at me.

"What happened, I was going to ask. That your husband's going to leave you."

"I told him I'm in love with somebody else. I have been for a while."

Sharla shouted from the kitchen. I couldn't hear what she wanted.

"The stupid thing is, I'm not even doing anything about it," Jade said.

I didn't say anything.

Jade's hands clenched and unclenched under the water. She looked at the fans her fingers made. "He's married."

You are, too, I thought.

"He doesn't know," Jade said. "I mean, the guy. I haven't told him. It's just hard."

She was staring at me, trying to tell me something in code.

I thought, it's Grady. She's trying to let me know.

But that was dumb. Grady had never even met Jade, as far as I knew.

But he might have, when he was on a course or something. Or at the hockey tournament. I couldn't go last year because I was pregnant and sick. I was pretty pissed off that Grady went, in fact. He got his mom to come and help me out while he was gone.

Sharla came back with a tray, carrying the police radio by its antenna. The radio was crackling again.

I could hear Ron. He was saying, "We'll be 10-77, you can reach us here."

In the radio code, 10-77 is *at home*.

Just as I figured that out, Ron put his head around the sunroom door. He grinned at us and waved. He said 10-4 into the small radio on his shoulder and clicked it off.

"Hey, ladies!" Ron said. "Grady, we picked the right time to come home! It's a strip show!"

Grady stuck his head around the door, like a cop checking the scene before entering. He can't help it. In a restaurant he always has to sit with his back against the wall.

"This is Jade, Tim Lamont's better half," Ron was telling Grady. "Really great you could make it, Jade—I thought you were stuck helping with the teen party?"

Sharla talked over him. "We found her at the hall. Did you guys even see us? I was right there on the dance floor when that all started."

Sharla was trying to cover up the mean thing she'd done, but it was too plain. She must have told Ron that Jade couldn't come. But really, she had never invited Jade.

Jade looked at Ron, then at Sharla. "I—no, it turns out. They went to Donna's, so they didn't need me."

Ron didn't seem to notice that Sharla had been mean. Or that Jade had figured out the truth and was playing along, being kind. Guys miss things. They expect everyone to be as straightforward as they are.

Grady had seen the truth, though. He didn't like Ron being fooled.

He passed Sharla and came to say hi to Jade.

"I know Tim from a course," he said.

Jade looked up--she had been staring down into the water.

"He taught the new member course when Ron and I were on it a couple of years ago. Good guy."

"Yeah," Jade said. "He likes teaching. Means a few weeks away from here."

"He's an excellent teacher," Grady said. He undid his parka. "Hot in here!"

Sharla hurried through. Her robe was coming open, showing the top of her pink chest.

"Now you can finally relax," she told Grady. She pressed a White Russian into his hand.

He took the glass but didn't drink.

Ron threw his coat on a chair. He undid his collar.

"Wish I could jump in there with you," he said to Jade. "Grady, you should peel off. Hey, Sharla, no drink for me?"

Sharla gave him a dirty look. She went back to the kitchen.

"What took you guys so long?" she called back.

"Had to wait for a guard. Those boys needed some Band-Aids, too," Ron said. He smiled at Jade. "Can't let their moms see them like that. Good thing your boys weren't in on the fight. I'd hate to have to deal with *their* mom later. I hear she's a firecracker."

Jade laughed, her face bright and happy. "'They only fight with each other. That's enough blood for me."

Daisy began to kick her legs and complain, reaching with her arms. She wanted to go to Grady. He heard her and came over. He lifted her up with his big hands and settled her in the crook of his arm. He didn't seem to mind the water getting on his shirt.

"Who's the baby?" he asked her. "Who's the baby girl?" Sap. Daisy loved it, though.

"We did meet," Jade said to Grady.

She smiled at him. Her teeth were as nice as Sharla's. But she was way better looking, I thought.

And way more Grady's type.

"We met at Moxie's, in Edmonton," Jade told him. "During the course. I went in a few times to have dinner with Tim. I remember you. And Ron."

Grady laughed. "I was in a daze, trying to remember what I'd been taught. Hoping not to screw up in front of Tim, probably."

Hearing about Grady being out with other people always makes me jealous. It's just because I hardly ever get to go.

But if I met him, I'd be in love with him. I mean, when I did meet him, I was. I am. I should not have had that drink, I thought. It's making me stupid.

"Who did your hair?" Grady asked me. "You look like Princess Buttercup at the wedding."

"Yeah, Robin Wright, *The Princess Bride!*" Sharla said. She had brought Ron's drink in from the kitchen. "She was my idol. I looked like her, back then."

She put down a platter of egg rolls and slid out of her robe and into the water like a bare pink fish. Sharla still looked like a princess, a lot more than I did, anyway.

"Sharla did my hair," I said. "She did a good job, eh?"

Grady looked at me over Daisy's head. He crossed his eyes.

"Oh, yeahhh," he said, in a voice that meant, *What the hell has she done to you? Where's my real wife?*

I laughed.

I stopped worrying. Jade was not in love with Grady. He wouldn't do that, let someone be in love with him.

Ron picked up his drink and sat on the edge of the hot tub between Jade and Sharla.

"So," he said. "When do I dare get out of this uniform and make you women happy?"

The radio jumped on the tray.

"Jinx," Grady said.

"We forgot to tell you, the buffalo got out again," I told him. We should have phoned Control. It hadn't occurred to me then. I didn't say anything about nearly getting mowed down.

Ron was already up and in his coat.

He moved fast, talking to the control room. An MVA—motor vehicle accident.

Grady gave me Daisy and his untouched drink, grabbed his coat, and went out the door with Ron. Daisy looked after him, lost and lonely.

"It's okay, baby," I told her. "He'll be back."

Ron turned and gave us a quick wave. I looked over at Sharla—she didn't look up from her egg roll.

But Jade was watching him go. Her face had the same look as Daisy's. Like she'd been left by her beloved.

Oh shit, I thought—and *thank goodness,* tangled up in the same thought. It's Ron.

Chapter Nine

Sharla's purple dress lay on the floor, where she'd dropped it when we first got into the hot tub. The sparkly necklace spread over it like fireworks.

Midnight must be close, I thought. *Please let midnight come soon,* so I can go to bed.

We had finished the egg rolls and more wings. The caramel apple pie oozed half-eaten on the edge of the tub.

Jade broke a fingernail getting a Diet Coke open. *Tsk,* went Sharla, sucking her teeth. She brought out her nail polish case. After she fixed Jade's nail, she painted all our nails and glued a little fake diamond on each tip. My hands looked like they belonged to somebody else. To Sharla, actually.

Jade and Sharla kept talking and talking while I stayed quiet.

If a person thinks she knows something, should she tell? And tell who, anyway—Sharla? Ron?

I could tell Grady, maybe, but he looks down on gossip. I could just keep quiet. I thought, too, about Sharla's three babies that didn't happen.

By then Jade and Sharla were deep into the high school teacher issue. Whether she really had a thing going on with some boy. Whether or not she would be fired, although they seemed to agree she *should* be.

Sharla was betting the teacher would be canned for sure. Jade said the story might just be wishful thinking by the students. Sharla snorted at that.

"I've seen her giving Ron the eye," Sharla said. "She should have her teaching licence taken away."

They got into a bit of a fight, in a mild way.

While they argued, I got out and found a diaper for Daisy. I sat on the edge of the tub to cool down a bit and let Daisy stay dry. I sang along to the music playing on the radio. Quietly,

quietly, me and Daisy alone together. The others didn't notice. I sipped my drink. Grady's drink.

"What do you think, Dixie?" Sharla said. She wanted someone on her side.

"About what?"

Sharla ground her teeth. "About the teacher!"

Daisy had drifted into sleep on my shoulder.

"I guess—I don't know. Does she love the guy?"

"I don't think that's the point," Sharla said sharply.

I stared at her. She was so pretty on the outside and so prickly on the inside.

"I think I am a bit drunk," I said. "Isn't love always the point?"

Jade shook her head. "Not to me, not if the boy was my son. If it's true, then it's *abuse* —"

But that wasn't what I meant. I talked faster.

"I mean, if she really loves the guy, she won't want to wreck his life. So she wouldn't sleep with him, because that would wreck his life."

They stared at me.

"If she *doesn't* love him, she might have slept with him. Abused him. Or just—told him she's in love with him, or something. Whatever really happened."

Hard to talk about a teacher I'd never seen. I kept imagining her: really beautiful, with long dark hair. And lonely.

"I remember high school," I said. "It's like a very small town. Hardly any possible men. You know, the drama teacher is gay, the principal is old... So the one good man seems like everything. Maybe he has a mean girlfriend. Or maybe he's just really decent, really kind, and she—maybe she does love him."

My strategy was not working. I had almost talked myself onto Jade's side.

"You can get carried away by that secret, the secret of loving somebody," I said. "She might feel like wrecking her own life, losing her kids—I mean, the school kids. The job."

Sharla stared at me, as if a fish had started to talk.

"I mean, what she feels isn't necessarily real love." I knew I wasn't making any sense.

Jade looked at her hands under the water. The fake diamonds on her nails glittered.

"Anyway, we don't know what happened," I said. "So we can't judge her."

I sounded like Grady.

I bent down and slid Daisy, fast asleep, into her car seat.

Then my arms felt so light.

"It's got to be midnight by now," I said. "Shouldn't we bang the pots and pans or sing?"

Sharla stood up in the water.

"It's so *hot* in here," she said. "I'm boiling. I need some air!"

She jumped out and pulled open the patio door.

Beyond the misted glass, the night outside had changed. It had warmed up, and the wind was gone. Clean snow lay over the back yard like a blank sheet of paper.

Jade got out, too. She went to the door. Steam rose in clouds off her long back and legs. "Oh, this is good," she said. "I needed this!"

She took a deep breath and then ran out onto the deck and down the stairs. She jumped full-length into the snow, face down.

Sharla gave a short scream, as if Jade was in danger.

Running into the snow looked like a really good idea to me.

I went past Sharla and out, walking barefoot through the snow. I'd been hot and sleepy for so long, I felt great. I slid down the deck steps and fell backwards into a patch of untouched snow.

The snow was so, so, so cold! It felt like burning on my skin. I flapped my arms and legs to make an angel.

Sharla was laughing her head off. The night was quiet. Her laughter crackled in the air. She said, "Oh, I can't, I can't!" But she did. She ran out into the snow. She had nothing on, she must have frozen instantly.

I stood up to check my snow angel. Not bad. My feet were numb. Jade flapped her legs and arms, too, and Sharla managed to flap once before she had to jump up and run back. I almost beat her back, to slide into the hot water again.

Jade came more slowly. Her skin was beet red in the blue light from the tub.

We thawed.

"Okay," Sharla said. "I'm putting coffee on. If those guys don't come back in fifteen minutes, I'm going to bed."

She hauled herself out one last time and went to the kitchen.

Jade said, "I didn't tell my husband who the guy is. The one I'm in love with."

I nodded.

"I had that much sense," she added.

I laughed.

After a minute, she said, "You were right to say what you did. I don't want to wreck Ron's life. Or mine."

She looked so sad I could hardly bear it.

"I think about leaving Grady all the time," I told her. "I have a list of what to pack."

She put her hand on my arm.

"I might be wrong," I said. "Maybe yours is real."

Jade shook her head. "No. I don't think so. Things aren't real until you… get together, until you are both… until you've talked to each other."

Sharla came back with a stack of pink towels.

"I guess the whole story is wishful thinking," Jade said.

Chapter Ten

Grady woke me up when he climbed into bed beside me.

"You smell good," he said.

"Hot tub and caramel apple pie," I said. "Now I know what hand cream to get."

"Look, I have a sensitive nose. I'll find you some caramel apple hand cream. Nice angels out there in the back yard. Must have been pretty cold, making them. Where's the baby?"

"Oops, I left her on the roof of the car..." That was our joke. "She's on the floor beside me. We made a bed for her with some rolled blankets. Hey, I gave her a bottle of formula. She did spit out the first few gulps. But then she got used to it."

"Well, about time," he said.

"Yeah. I'll nurse her again in the morning after this buzz has worn off. Good to have the option of a bottle though. You were right."

He sighed and curved his legs behind mine. We lay still for a while.

"What was that last thing?" I asked him.

"The accident? A truck spun out and clipped an SUV. Both totalled."

"I was worried that it was the buffalo. That caused the accident, I mean."

"Nope. Those buffalo are off into the hills by now. They go where they want, ignore everything else. That rancher lost one before, a couple of years ago. Never saw it again."

"Was the accident bad?" I was afraid to ask. Finding people badly injured, or a dead person, was hard on him.

"Nobody died," he said. "Just hurt feelings and glass all over the place."

We were quiet for a minute.

"You were out for a long time, though."

"We just drove around all night. Ron didn't want to come home."

I tried to imagine what they would talk about, driving around.

"I always want to come home," Grady said. He slid his arm under my head. "He's having a hard time here, with Tim in Vegas and Marie on sick leave with her broken leg. He says Marie's a great Mountie, that's one good thing. But he seems pretty depressed."

I waited. He didn't continue. I thought he might have fallen asleep.

Grady's pretty depressed himself. I know that. And when things are bad, he finds talking hard. Sometimes days and days go by before he tells me about things. Before we're in the same bed at the same time. And both awake—that hardly ever happens any more.

I go a bit crazy when we don't talk.

"I think about leaving you all the time," I said, softly in case he was sleeping. "I have a plan. What to take, where to pack things in the suitcases."

"Don't think about that," Grady said in the darkness. "Don't leave."

We lay quiet.

"I think about quitting my job all the time," he said, after a few minutes. "But I can't quit, there's the baby."

"Why don't you ever call her by her name?"

He didn't answer.

Because he hates her name. I knew that for sure now. I kicked myself. I shouldn't have asked him then, when he was talking about quitting. He *should* quit. Get out of this crazy police life before it grinds him too far down.

"Maybe I'm still getting used to her," he said. "Anyway. Fuck it. Go back to sleep, Princess Buttercup. And Daisy. My flowers."

Chapter Eleven

In the morning, we drove away.

Daisy was safe in her car seat after nursing again. The formula hadn't killed her.

Ron came out on the front deck to wave. Sharla was still sleeping off last night's shooters.

Grady waved back. He rolled the window up quick once we got going.

"Nice visit," Grady said.

"Nobody died," I said. He laughed.

It was still pretty cold. Snow had stopped falling. The sun shone high and white. Today was a new year.

"I know where I belong, and nothing's gonna happen," Grady sang.

He has the best voice. I love when he sings. It means he is okay. We are okay.

"She's so high, high above me, she's so lovely."

Daisy watched his face in the rear-view mirror, bright eyes brimming with sadness or laughter. She was too young for us to know which it was.

The wind had cleared the road. It had blown away the hoof prints of the buffalo and the snow stained with blood from last night's fight. Where the accident had been, I saw broken glass heaped beside the ditch.

Loose snow blew in long strands across the road. They made a new white road following the line of the wind.

I love that sideways road that the wind takes. It ignores everything except what it really wants. It shows where we ought to be going, which is not very often where we are going.

The wind's road is where I want us to go.

Good Reads

Discover Canada's Bestselling Authors with Good Reads Books

Good Reads authors have a special talent—
the ability to tell a great story, using clear language.

Good Reads books are ideal for people

＊ on the go, who want a short read;

＊ who want to experience the joy of reading;

＊ who want to get into the reading habit.

To find out more, please visit
www.GoodReadsBooks.com

The Good Reads project is sponsored by
ABC Life Literacy Canada.

The project is funded in part by the Government of Canada's
Office of Literacy and Essential Skills.

Libraries and literacy and education markets
order from Grass Roots Press.

Bookstores and other retail outlets order from HarperCollins Canada.

Good Reads Series

If you enjoyed this Good Reads book,
you can find more at your local library or bookstore.

✳

The Stalker by Gail Anderson-Dargatz

In From the Cold by Deborah Ellis

Home Invasion by Joy Fielding

The Day the Rebels Came to Town by Robert Hough

Picture This by Anthony Hyde

Missing by Frances Itani

Shipwreck by Maureen Jennings

The Picture of Nobody by Rabindranath Maharaj

The Hangman by Louise Penny

Easy Money by Gail Vaz-Oxlade

✳

For more information on Good Reads,
visit **www.GoodReadsBooks.com**

The Day the Rebels Came to Town

By Robert Hough

The year is 1920, and all of Mexico is at war with itself. Gangs of rebels roam the country, stealing money, food, and horses. Carlos is twenty-eight years old. He works in his father's café. One day, a gang rides into Carlos's village. When the gang leaves, they kidnap Carlos.

Weeks later, the rebels and Carlos ride into the town of Rosita. Suddenly, Carlos is forced to make a life or death decision. He does so, though in a way that surprises everyone.

Is Carlos a brave man or a coward? It is a question that takes him a lifetime to answer.

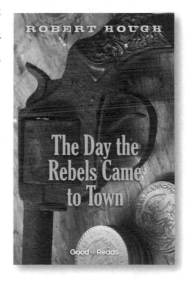

Missing
By Frances Itani

Missing is based on a true story.

Luc Caron lives in northern France during World War I. One day, he sees three airplanes fighting in the sky. Luc watches in horror as a plane flips over and the pilot falls to his death. Luc is the only witness.

The Greenwoods own an apple farm in Canada. Their son, a pilot, has been missing for 11 years. In 1928, they receive a package from England. The package contains a letter and three

objects found at the site of a plane crash.

How is the mystery of the missing pilot solved, bringing peace to Luc and to the pilot's parents?

Home Invasion

By Joy Fielding

Kathy Brown suddenly wakes up. Was that a noise in the house, or part of her dream?

In her dream, Kathy was about to kiss Michael, her high school boyfriend. Her husband, Jack, lies beside her, snoring. Michael is exciting. Jack is boring.

When Kathy hears the noise again, she gets up. Then she hears whispers. Then she feels a gun at her head. Two men are in the house. Kathy and her husband face a living nightmare. Kathy must also face her real feelings about her husband.

The outcome surprises everyone, most of all Kathy herself.

About the Author

 Marina Endicott is the bestselling author of *Good to a Fault*. This book was a finalist for the Giller Prize and a *Globe and Mail* Best Book. Her latest book, *The Little Shadows*, follows a singing sister act touring the prairies in 1912.

Marina worked as an actor and director before she began to write fiction. She currently teaches creative writing at the University of Alberta. Marina lives in Edmonton with her husband (a Royal Canadian Mounted Police officer), two children, and one small dog.

Also by Marina Endicott:

Open Arms
Good to a Fault
The Little Shadows

*